Me and My Dragon
Christmas Spirit

David Biedrzycki

ini Charlesbridge

Published by Charlesbridge
85 Main Street
Watertown, MA 02472
(617) 926-0329
www.charlesbridge.com

Library of Congress Cataloging-in-Publication Data
Biedrzycki, David, author, illustrator.
    Me and my dragon : Christmas spirit / written and
illustrated by David Biedrzycki.
        p. cm.
    Summary: A boy and his pet dragon discover the meaning
of the Christmas spirit.
    ISBN 978-1-58089-622-1 (reinforced for library use)
    ISBN 978-1-60734-907-5 (ebook)
    ISBN 978-1-60734-908-2 (ebook pdf)
1. Christmas stories. 2. Dragons—Juvenile fiction.
3. Pets—Juvenile fiction. 4. Generosity—Juvenile fiction.
[1. Christmas—Fiction. 2. Dragons—Fiction. 3. Pets—
Fiction. 4. Generosity—Fiction.] I. Title.
PZ7.B4745Mf 2015
[E]—dc23   2014010496

Printed in China
(hc) 10 9 8 7 6 5 4 3 2 1

Illustrations done in Adobe Photoshop
Display type set in Jellygest by Jakob Fischer at
    www.pizzadude.dk, and Metro Script by Michael Doret/
    Alphabet Soup Type
Text type set in Providence Sans by Guy Jeffrey
    Nelson, FontShop International
Color separations by Colourscan Print Co Pte Ltd, Singapore
Printed by C & C Offset Printing Co. Ltd. in Shenzhen,
    Guangdong, China
Production supervision by Brian G. Walker
Designed by Diane M. Earley

To Mary Parrish, Amber Jackson,
Linda Staenberg, Laura Wright,
Laura McLaughlin, Cecilia Cordeiro,
and the Winchester Authorfest

My pet dragon is the best
friend a kid could have.

But he doesn't understand what the Christmas spirit is all about. I do.

I know Christmas is about giving.

Give to Others

I want
a bike—
a BIG bike!

and spreading joy to those around us.

I don't think Dragon has a clue about any of this.

We needed to make some cash.

But there aren't many jobs for a little kid and a dragon. We were going to have to get creative.

Help Wanted

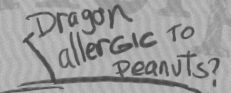

Dragon allergic to peanuts?

Dragon gets seasick!

Dragon scared of robots

Peanut-Butter Taster
If you think you're a peanut-butter expert, this job is for you. Give us your opinion on crunchy, smooth, or organic brands. Milk and bread included. Call 555-5555.

Santa's Helper
Apply at the North Pole. Ask for Rudolph.

Ghost Finder

Part-Time Pirate
Only lovers of the high seas need apply. Duties include swabbing the deck, dropping anchor, rigging the sails, and saying "Arrghh!" Apply at Pier 92 before dawn.

Alligator Dentist
We're looking for a replacement to our staff. Applicants must be brave and very quick. Must relocate to Florida. Apply at our Alligator Alley Office.

Robot Mechanic
Applicants must know all about robots mechanics and pro

Tooth-Fairy Assistant
Work part-time nights. Must have w knowledge of reading dental records

Teacher's Pet
First-grade teacher looking for a pet. No dog cats, or bunnies, please. Applicants must brin apple to class and smile a lot.

Shark Feeder
Loo aquarium seeks responsible an rienced scuba diver to s. Life insurance

Dragon landed a job at the Burger Barn broiling burgers. They were all cooked well-done.

EDDIE'S TEDDIES

Toasted
Marshmallow
on a Stick
50¢

CHRISTMAS TREES DELIVERED

We took all the odd jobs
we could get.

Me and my dragon were a money-making machine!

We even had time to babysit Mrs. Jones's seven kids—for free—while she went food shopping. Brrr, her house was cold.

It was time to buy our presents. Dragon and I split the money.

On my way to the store, I thought of something. My tummy was full, and our house was warm. Me and my dragon have everything we need.

But not everybody does.

Christmas morning was warm and toasty at our house. I gave everyone portraits I had made. I thought they looked pretty good.

Wow! This is . . . GREAT, son!

Mom and Dad gave me a new sword and shield.

Dragon made cookies.

But then Dragon surprised us.
He had some presents that he
wanted to deliver . . .

together.